The After Christmas Tree

A book to share from
Scallywag Press

In memory of my dad, Brian

First published in Great Britain in 2020
by Scallywag Press Ltd, 10 Sutherland Row, London SW1V 4JT

Text and illustration copyright © Bethan Welby, 2020
The rights of Bethan Welby to be identified as the author and illustrator
of this work have been asserted by her in accordance with the
Copyright, Designs and Patents Act, 1988

Printed on FSC paper in China by Toppan Leefung

001

British Library Cataloguing in Publication Data available
ISBN 978–1–912650–39–2

The After Christmas Tree

Bethan Welby

Scallywag Press Ltd
LONDON

It was a grey day in January.

A Christmas tree sat outside by the road,
wondering why no one was smiling
at her any more.

Brian was wondering the same thing.

"Don't worry,
tree.

I'll look after you,
I promise . . .

You can come home
with me!"

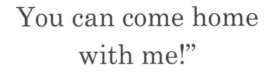

At tea time Brian set a place for the tree at the table.

Only Brian was smiling.

Afterwards, everyone sat on the sofa to watch T.V.

Only Brian was smiling.

Then it was bath time.

"Mum!"

By bedtime Brian and the Christmas tree were both anxious and unhappy.

Nobody was smiling.

"That tree is going to have to go outside," said Mum.
"Would you like me to help you?"

"No," said Brian quietly. "I'll do it.
It's my tree."

Brian tossed and turned, remembering his promise to look after the little tree.

He couldn't stop worrying about it,
bare and alone in the cold, snowy night.

But when his eyes closed at last,
he dreamt a magical dream . . .

The next morning Brian got up and looked out of the window.

"Oh . . . !"

The tree wasn't bare
or lonely at all!

Everyone came running –
and *everyone* was smiling!

And when Christmas came again?

Well . . . Brian picked up the little tree
and took it back inside the house.